GUINEA PIGS ONLINE VIKING VICTORY

By Jennifer Gray and Amanda Swift

Guinea Pigs Online

Furry Towers

GUINEA PIGS ONLINE VIKING VICTORY

Jennifer Gray & Amanda Swift

Illustrations by Sarah Horne

Quercus

New York • London

Quercus

New York • London

© 2013 by Jennifer Gray and Amanda Swift
Illustrations © 2013 by Sarah Horne
First published in the United States by Quercus in 2014

ISBN 978-1-62365-347-7

Library of Congress Control Number: 2013913488

Distributed in the United States and Canada by
Random House Publisher Services
c/o Random House, 1745 Broadway
New York, NY 10019

Manufactured in the United States

2 4 6 8 10 9 7 5 3 1

www.quercus.com

For Philippa and Rhea
J.G.

For Dan and Tom
A.S.

For my brother Oliver, with love
S.H.

contents

1
The Monster Machine

Some days are exciting. Some days are boring. And some days are exciting, boring, funny, scary, tiring, and—if they involve juicy green grass—delicious, especially if you're a guinea pig. For Fuzzy, Coco, and Eduardo, this day started out boring. Well, it was boring for Coco, because Terry, the techno-whiz-kid from next door, was teaching Fuzzy how to fix the TV remote control. And all Coco wanted to do was talk about the new bow she'd gotten for her hair.

"First you need to check if the batteries have run out," instructed Terry.

"OK," said Fuzzy.

"Then you need to check if the signal is broken," Terry continued.

"OK," said Fuzzy.

"It also helps if it's the right remote

control," added Coco. "That's the one for the CD player."

"I can make any remote control work anything," said Terry proudly.

"Well, excuse me for trying to be helpful," said Coco, looking out the window. She suddenly flung herself onto the pile of cushions the guinea pigs had used to bounce onto the sofa. Then she raced across the living room carpet, along the landing, wriggled backward down the stairs into the kitchen, scuttled across the floor, and was just about to leap out of the cat flap when it was shoved open from the

outside. A red
scooter ridden
by a handsome
silver-and-black
guinea pig
landed on
the doormat,
on top of Coco.

"You could have knocked," said
Coco, picking herself up.

"Señor-ita," panted Eduardo.
"I—no—time—have—for—the—
knocking." He gasped between each
word.

"Could you breathe *or* talk, instead

5

of doing both quite badly at the same time," she chattered impatiently. Eduardo didn't seem to have noticed her new bow either.

Coco had a bad habit of sometimes being mean to people she really loved. She was mean to Fuzzy, her hutch-mate, she was mean to Eduardo, whom she secretly liked, and sometimes she was even mean to the Queen, with whom she used to live at Buckingham Palace.

Eduardo started babbling in Spanish because he didn't have time to figure out what he wanted to say in English. (Eduardo spoke Spanish because he was from Peru.)

"Whoa, slow down!" Fuzzy had come down to the kitchen with Terry to find out what was going on. Eduardo repeated what he had just said, this time in English.

"In the thicket there is a huge monster!" Eduardo lived in a cozy burrow in the thicket at the bottom of Fuzzy and Coco's garden.

"It is eating my house!" Eduardo started to say that the monster was yellow and black, but the other guinea pigs didn't hear because they had

dived out of the cat flap almost as
fast as Eduardo and his scooter had
dived in.

"That's not a monster, it's a digger!"
said Fuzzy when the guinea pigs

arrived at the thicket. "Haven't you ever watched the Digger Channel?"

What Fuzzy hadn't expected, though, was to see a digger crashing over the flowers and ferns of their beloved thicket. This shouldn't happen! The thicket was a quiet place. The loudest noise they'd ever heard out there apart from Eduardo singing was a butterfly's burp.

BURRP!!

Now there came a noise even louder than the digger's engine: "Right, dude. I'll make a start tomorrow. I'll have this place cleared before you can say sausage sandwich."

It was a human voice. The guinea pigs looked up. Just above the giant rubber wheels of the digger, in the cab of the monster machine, sat a little round man with red cheeks, shouting into his cellphone:

"I reckon I

could fit half a dozen houses on here."

"Half a dozen!" exclaimed Fuzzy. "There's not even room for ten."

Math was not Fuzzy's strong point.

"Half a dozen is six," said Coco kindly, because she *was* kind most of the time.

"Even one house is too many," said Eduardo sadly, scooting up to join them.

"Too right," said Fuzzy, stamping his paw.

"Ow," said Coco, because he had accidentally stamped on *her* paw.

"Sorry! We need to do something about this," said Fuzzy.

"We're too small," said Eduardo. "Even I, Eduardo Julio Antonio del Monte, freedom fighter from the mighty mountains of Peru, cannot fight the giant metal machine."

"Maybe not," said Fuzzy. "But we can tell others. We can get help."

"Leave it to me," said Coco. "I'll go next door and have a word with your mom, Terry." Terry's mom, Banoffee, lived next door with Terry and her thirteen other kids. Coco and Banoffee were friends. Banoffee was also great at doing Coco's hair and was bound to notice her new bow. "She can tell your brothers and sisters, and they'll tell their friends, and they'll tell their parents, and before long you'll have reached all the guinea pigs in Strawberry Park."

"Good idea—*not!*" said Terry. He pulled his woolly hat down over his ears. "We could just put something about it on the Internet and reach about six billion guinea pigs instead. That's it!" he cried. "We can organize a protest. It'll be mega!"

Coco glared at him. She wasn't very keen on computers. She preferred talking.

"I've got an idea," said Fuzzy, who didn't want to upset either of them. "Let's try both!"

2
Blogging On

"We need to start a blog," said Terry.

Back at number 7 Middleton

Crescent the guinea pigs sat on a

purple yoga mat in front of a laptop.

The yoga mat belonged to Henrietta,

who was Coco's owner; the laptop

belonged to Ben, who was Fuzzy's

owner. Henrietta had bought the
yoga mat thinking she would be good
at yoga, and Ben had bought the
laptop thinking he would be good
at computer games. But usually it
was Henrietta who played games on
the laptop while Ben lay on the mat
waving his legs in the air.

"What's a bog?" Coco asked,
getting up and practicing her yoga
stretches. "I thought it was a toilet?"

"Not a bog, a blog!" Fuzzy said
kindly. Coco really didn't know much
about computers.

"It's an online diary," Terry

explained. "You tell guinea pigs what's really happening in the world so they can get together and help stop bad things. It's like tweeting," he added, "but longer."

"Tweeting?" Eduardo's bushy eyebrows knitted together in a frown. "Like my amigos the Peruvian songbirds?" He laughed. "Next, my friend, you will be telling me this computer can fly."

Terry and Fuzzy looked at each other.

"Never mind," Terry said, tapping away at the keys. "Check this out." He pointed at the screen:

"One likes the title," Coco puffed, forgetting for a moment she wasn't at

Buckingham Palace, where she had learned to say "one" instead of "you" or "I." "But one doesn't want any guinea pigs being sick on one's new bow." She twiddled it, hoping someone would notice.

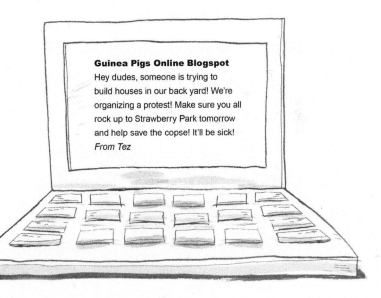

Guinea Pigs Online Blogspot
Hey dudes, someone is trying to build houses in our back yard! We're organizing a protest! Make sure you all rock up to Strawberry Park tomorrow and help save the copse! It'll be sick!
From Tez

"It's not that sort of sick," Fuzzy explained. "It means 'fantastic'!"

"Well, why doesn't it say so then?" Coco grumbled. She got up and tried to stand on one leg like she'd seen Ben do, which is hard if you're a guinea pig, because you need at least two to balance. "And who's Tez?"

"Me!" Terry explained. "It's kids' slang: like 'sick.'" He sniggered. "You need to lighten up, Co."

"It's Coco, actually!" Coco was so upset he'd made her name sound less fancy that she fell over.

"Wait, I have something even more

sicker, Señor Tez!" Eduardo cried. He jumped onto the laptop and clattered up and down the keys; then hopped off with a low bow. "My latest song," he said modestly. "I just made it up."

Guinea Pigs Online Songblong
Guinea pigs of the world, unite!
Against the baddies we will fight.
Let's stop the houses, save the copse,
Bite the builder, rip his socks!
Amigos, come to Strawberry Park tomorrow,
Please to help me save my burrow!
Edz

"OK, now I've got one." Coco picked herself up and nipped onto the keyboard.

"Let's try all three," sighed Fuzzy. He put on his chef's hat. (Fuzzy

Guinea Pigs Online Bogspog
One demands the presence of Her Majesty's loyal guinea-pig subjects tomorrow at one's royal copse to help one's friends.
Coco
(In case you were wondering why I'm so posh, I used to live with the Queen.)

liked to cook.) "I'll rustle up a little something in the kitchen while we wait to see who's going to join the protest."

3
Ping!

ing!

"That's one reply." Coco munched on some broccoli.

Ping!

"That's two." Eduardo crunched on some carrots.

Ping!

"That's three." Fuzzy burped
through a mouthful of avocado.

Ping! Ping! Ping! Ping! Ping!
Ping! Ping! Ping! Ping! Ping!
Ping! Ping! Ping! Ping! Ping!
Ping! Ping! Ping! Ping! Ping!
Ping! Ping! Ping!

"And that's a whole lot more!" Terry finished his celery and approached the screen. "I told you it would work."

"One's bogspog was obviously a big hit!" Coco said, taking the credit.

"Uh-uh," Eduardo jumped in, "my songblong was an international sensation."

"No, bros," Terry complained. "My blog was totally out there."

"You all did very well," Fuzzy said.

"I did the best," Coco insisted.

"No, señorita," said Eduardo, "I think you'll find I did."

"No way!" Terry said. "I'm the coolest."

Fuzzy sighed.

"We'll see about that!" Coco cried.

"You're on!" Terry yelled.

PING!

"Who's that from?" Eduardo demanded. "Let's ask *them* who they think is the best blonger."

The guinea pigs peered at the screen.

"Hello, little pigs, it's Renard the guinea pig. I'd like to join your protest. I live in the thicket too and I want to save it."

"Wait a minute," Coco cried. "Last time I got an e-mail from a guinea pig named Renard, he turned out to be the fox!"

"That's exactly what I was thinking," Fuzzy said. "Let's see if we can find out who it really is."

"What do you look like?" he typed. He winked at Eduardo. **"So we can recognize you and say hello."**

"Ah, amigo, that is very cunning," Eduardo said admiringly.

Another message appeared on the screen.

"I am orange and have big pointy ears."

The guinea pigs looked at one another. They knew a few guinea pigs with orange splotches on their fur but none with big pointy ears.

"That's unusual for a guinea pig," Fuzzy wrote.

There was a pause.

"Yes, that is because I am a very rare type of guinea pig."

"I bet it's him," Coco whispered, although she didn't need to because whoever it was couldn't hear her down the computer.

"What type are you?" Fuzzy wrote.

"Er . . . the big-eared bushy-tailed variety."

"Gotcha!" Fuzzy cried.

Eduardo fell over laughing. "*Caramba*, that fox is stupid. Everyone knows guinea pigs don't have tails!"

"What if he comes tomorrow, though?" Coco sounded worried. "He'll eat us all!" Coco had nearly been eaten by the fox on two occasions.

"I'll biff him in the snout," Eduardo boasted.

"Maybe he's changed," Fuzzy suggested. "I mean, the fox lives in the thicket too. Maybe he really wants to help so he can save his home, like Eduardo."

The other guinea pigs hadn't thought of that.

"Let's ask him," Terry said. He got on to the keyboard.

"Look, pal, we know who you are so stop trying to be clever. Do you want to help us or not? Because if you only want to eat us, then we'll have to call the whole thing off. And then the builder will move in and you'll get thrown out on your tail."

"Nicely put, Señor Tez," Eduardo said.

It took only a few seconds for the reply to come back.

"OK, you got me. I am the fox, but I

promise I won't eat you. All I want to do is save the thicket! Otherwise I'll have to live on the railway line and eat nettles."

"Should we give him another chance?" Fuzzy wondered.

"We could do with his help," Terry said.

"Poor thing," Coco sighed, trying to think what the Queen would do. "One hates to think of one's subjects living on railway lines." She gave a little royal wave, then frowned. "What's the matter, Eduardo?"

Eduardo was staring at them, amazed. "You really trust that sneaky

lowlife fox?" He whistled. "Man, you pet cavies are crazy! It's lucky you have me to look after you at the protest."

"We can look after ourselves, thank you very much!" Coco shouted.

"Sure, señorita." Eduardo jumped

back on the scooter. "But if you don't mind, I think I'll go and get my *bolas* ready just in case."

"What are they?"

"Traditional Peruvian weapons, señorita. Wait and see."

Coco sighed. Eduardo could be annoying, but at least the day hadn't turned out boring after all. And tomorrow promised to be even more exciting!

4
guinea pigs United

The next morning Coco woke up early. She was feeling excited. Today was the day of the protest! Fuzzy was still snoozing in his corner of the hutch, so Coco decided to go out to the thicket on her own. She was looking forward to seeing lots of guinea pigs there. On the way out, she looked in the mirror. She pinched the ends of her fur to make it look spikier and maybe even a bit scary. That builder would get a fright when he saw hundreds of guinea pigs chattering at him! He'd soon change his plans . . .

When Coco arrived in the thicket the first thing she saw was a pinecone flying through the air and smashing into a tree.

"Who threw that?" asked Coco testily. "It's dangerous to throw things around. It could have hit me on the head, or even knocked my bow out of my fur," she said, checking it was still in place.

"It was Eduardo," said a girl guinea pig's voice that Coco didn't recognize. "Hello, I'm Sunbeam." The owner of the voice popped her head out from behind the tree. Well, it might have been her head: Coco wasn't sure. It might just as well have been her bottom! She had lots of very long black fur, and it was difficult to tell one end from the other.

"You don't look like a sunbeam, more like a moon crater," Coco muttered rudely.

But then a paw
appeared and the
guinea pig pushed
back her fur to
reveal a very
pretty yellow
face. "Eduardo's
brilliant, isn't he?"
said Sunbeam.

"Not really,"
said Coco.
She knew that wasn't a very nice
thing to say, but there was something
about this new girl that made her feel
grumpy.

"*Hombre, hombre,*" Eduardo muttered as he appeared from behind the tree and picked up the smashed pinecone from the ground. "These are useless."

"Is that your weapon?" asked Coco, gazing at the bits of string and the pinecones Eduardo held in his paw.

"That *was* my weapon," said Eduardo sadly. "I

did not bring the real *bolas* with me from Peru. They are meant to be made of wood and tied together with braided leather. There was not room in my satchel. So I made the *bolas* here in the thicket. But they are not strong enough. The *bolas* back home can stop a runaway horse at fifty meters. This *bolas* could not even stop a mouse at fifty centimeters."

He flung the bits of string with the remaining couple of pinecones on the end around his head, like a lasso. Then he threw them at a holly bush, where they immediately got stuck. He

tried to pull them out but the string
fell off.

"Maybe if you used something
heavier than pinecones . . ." said
Coco, going over to look more closely
at the broken weapon.

As soon as her back was turned,
Eduardo suddenly burst into song.

Guinea pigs of the world, unite!
Against the baddies we will fight.
Let's stop the houses, save the thicket,
Bite the builder, rip his socks!
Guinea pigs of the world, unite!
All the baddies we will fight.

Sunbeam joined in. When they finished she smiled sweetly. "Oh, Eduardo," she said, "that's such a wonderful protest song. Can we sing it again?"

"Of course, *chiquita*," Eduardo smiled back, and they began the song all over again.

Coco felt all sad inside because she had thought Eduardo was her special friend but now it looked like Sunbeam was his special friend. Sunbeam wasn't Coco's special friend; so it seemed that Sunbeam and Eduardo were both special to each other and she wasn't special at all.

She interrupted them singing. "Excuse me," she said loudly, "but could you shut up?"

Eduardo and Sunbeam stopped singing and looked at her.

Coco didn't feel right. She knew she wasn't being very nice, but she couldn't stop herself. "We have a protest to do. We can't just stand around singing," she said bossily.

"But we are protesting," argued Sunbeam. "We are singing Eduardo's brilliant protest song."

"Ladies, ladies," said Eduardo,

"perhaps we could sing the song together."

"No, thanks. I've got more important things to do," muttered Coco, and marched off on her own. "They're so busy singing to each other they haven't even noticed that no one else has showed up," she said to herself grumpily.

Coco was right. Where *were* all the guinea pigs who had promised to join the protest? She decided to go over to the main gate, which was the official way into the thicket from the street, and look for them.

As she approached the gate she slowed down. Something was wrong. It was quiet. There was no one around. Not a human, not a guinea pig, not a mouse, not even a worm. Then she heard a little shuffling noise from the street. *Shuffle, shuffle, shuffle.*

And in front of the gate appeared an elderly brown guinea pig with white whiskers.

At last! A supporter for their protest! The guinea pig lowered his head to squeeze under the gate. Coco moved forward to help him, but before she had taken a step there was a sudden movement from the laurel bush. A large red furry beast leaped forward and lunged at the protester. It was the fox! So much for wanting to help! He was the same Renard, up to his old tricks. That was why nobody had made it to the protest. He must have scared them off.

"Run! Run!" Coco cried. The elderly guinea pig looked startled and pulled back from the gate. Coco knew what would happen next. Renard would give up on catching him and try to catch her—again. She turned around and raced back to warn the others. All the jealousy she'd felt just a few minutes earlier had been forgotten. Guinea pigs had to stick together to fight the enemy, be it a fox or a digger. Or, in this case, both!

5
Digging In

*C*HUG CHUG CHUG CHUG
CHUG! There was a roar from the other
side of the main gate. The roar was
followed by a horrible scraping sound.

Coco froze. Renard the fox raced
toward her, but instead of eating her,
he went straight past and disappeared

into the bushes.

Then she knew for sure. The digger had returned!

"Quick, Coco!" Fuzzy appeared and grabbed her paw. "We need to start the protest!"

They scurried to where the other guinea pigs were waiting. Coco was relieved to see that there were a few more of them than before.

"Cooee!" It was Banoffee. "I brought the kids for a day out! We thought we'd have a picnic."

The extra guinea pigs were all her children!

"But, Banoffee," Coco said, "this could be dangerous!"

"Oh!" Banoffee looked confused.

"No, Mom, it'll be fine," Terry reassured her. "As soon as the builder sees us standing up to him, he'll back off."

"And then we can have our picnic!" Banoffee said cheerfully. "I brought bananas as a treat for when we win. They're nice and soggy. With black spots on them."

Banoffee's children all started squeaking with excitement at the prospect.

Coco hoped Banoffee and Terry were right. Not about the bananas being soggy, although that would be good, but that the protest would be over quickly and the builder would go away.

"Over here!" Eduardo and Sunbeam were hiding inside a thicket

beside a
mound of
mud. The
mound
was taller
than the
guinea pigs
and hidden from the builder's view
by the dense tangle of twigs, leaves,
and grass.

"I've never seen that here before."
Fuzzy scratched the crest on his head.
"I didn't know there were any mud
hills in the thicket."

"Pah!" Eduardo said. "Call that

a mud hill? You should see the mud mountains of Peru."

They could hear the sound of running water. It was coming from somewhere behind the mound of mud.

"I've never heard that here before, either." Fuzzy frowned. "I didn't know there was a river in the thicket."

"Pah!" Eduardo said. "Call that a

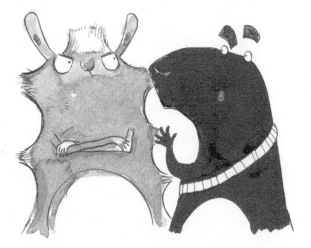

river? You should hear the giant rivers of the Andes. That is a stream."

"Shall we get on with it?" Coco said. "Or do you two want to argue about geography all day?"

They peered through the dense undergrowth. The digger had come to a halt just inside the gate. The little round man in the cab of the digger was shouting on his phone again.

"I'll start at the back. Away from the houses. That way I'll have cleared the trees before anyone notices. Everyone will be at work anyway." The builder sniggered. "By the time they get back tonight, this place will be as flat as a pancake, and it'll be too late for anyone to complain."

The guinea pigs chattered angrily. They knew how flat pancakes were—Fuzzy sometimes made them, sprinkled with a little fresh grass from the thicket. But if the builder got his way, there'd be no grass left in the thicket to sprinkle! There'd be no thickets, no laurel bushes, and no oak tree either. There wouldn't be a mud hill, or a river. And Eduardo's burrow would be a twisted pile of roots.

The builder put his phone away.

He got down out of his cab, pulled a map from his pocket, and started trudging around, crossing things out on the map with a pencil.

"The only good thing about plants," he chortled, "is digging them up!"

"If only my *bolas* was working properly," said Eduardo, shaking his fist, "I'd dig *you* up!"

The builder wandered toward the guinea pigs' hiding place. "Might as well start here!" he said, letting out an enormous burp. A horrible smell of half-digested sausage sandwich and stale tea wafted toward them.

Coco nearly fainted.

Sunbeam actually did. She keeled over on her back with her legs in the air.

"She needs the kiss of life!" Eduardo sprang forward.

Fuzzy tried to push in front of him. "I know first aid!" he said.

Coco got there first. "There's no need for any of that!" she squealed. "Banoffee, you stay with Sunbeam. The rest of you, come with me!"

The guinea pigs squeezed out of the thicket.

The builder had gotten back into the cab. He was revving the digger up.

CHUG CHUG CHUG CHUG CHUG! The machine roared.

"Form a line!" Coco ordered.

"Are you sure this is a good idea?" Fuzzy whispered. The digger looked even bigger than the ones on the Digger Channel.

"Well, I don't know, do I?" Coco said testily. "It was your idea."

"No, it wasn't—it was Terry's."

"Trust me," Terry had joined them. He pulled his woolly hat down firmly. "As soon as he sees us, he'll give up. I've seen it on TV."

"Yes, but that's with people, not guinea pigs," Fuzzy said nervously. "What if he *doesn't* see us?"

"*Caramba*, that thing is big!" Eduardo said.

The digger lurched forward. The scoop began to descend.

"Maybe we need to jump up and

down a bit," Terry suggested. His skinny knees were knocking. "And wave."

The guinea pigs jumped up and down and waved.

"It's not making any difference!" Fuzzy gulped.

The digger trundled toward them.

The scoop was like a giant fox's mouth waiting to gobble them up.

"I'm out of here!" Terry yelped. "Come on, everyone!" He disappeared, followed by his brothers and sisters.

"Me too!" Fuzzy scuttled off.

"I need to get my *bolas* working!" Eduardo chased after Fuzzy into the thicket.

Only Coco held her ground. Surely the builder would notice her beautiful new pink bow and scary spiky fur. And then surely he would stop the digger.

Suddenly she felt a pair of paws around her middle.

"You too, señorita!" Eduardo dragged her back into the undergrowth.

The scoop munched its way through the tangled plants toward the mud hill.

The guinea pigs covered their eyes. It was all over!

CRUNCH! The scoop hit something hard.

The digger juddered to a halt. The engine had stalled!

From inside the cab, the builder shouted a lot of very rude words.

Luckily the guinea pigs didn't understand any of them. He got back on his phone.

"The blasted thing's jammed!" he shouted. "I'm going to have to go back to the scrapyard to get some parts." He got down out of the cab and burped again. "And another sausage sandwich. With a fried egg on it this time. I'm starving!"

6
Olaf the Viking

"By the might of Odin, it's raining mud!" an angry voice shouted.

All the guinea pigs hiding in the thicket looked around. The voice didn't sound as if it had come from any of them.

"By the wrath of Thor, I'm going

to need a bath tonight!" came the voice.

The guinea pigs looked around again. Everyone's mouth was shut, except Banoffee's youngest, who had a blocked nose.

"By the teeth of Loki, I can't see my feet!"

This time the guinea pigs knew. The voice was coming from behind the mud hill. Eduardo was the first to move. "Leave this to me," he said, as he scurried up the hill at great speed.

When he got to the top he looked over the other side. What he saw was

surprising: it was a light
brown guinea pig with
woolly fur and
horns!

The strange
guinea pig started
shouting again:
"By the ant
of Adam, stay
right there, or I'll
slice you with my
sword!"

Eduardo looked at the weapon the
guinea pig was swinging around in
the air. It looked like a twig.

"*Hombre*, I come in peace,"
Eduardo shouted down. "I am an
Agouti guinea pig from Peru. Who
are you?"

"I am a Viking guinea pig from
the year 892," the horned guinea pig
shouted back.

Caramba! That was old! Eduardo
reckoned he could beat him in a fight,
especially as the Viking only had a
twig as a weapon.

"What's going on?" Coco shouted up.

"I'm going down," Eduardo said.
"Stay there until I come get you."

Sunbeam had woken up. "Are you

sure it's safe?" she asked in a worried voice.

"I'll be fine," said Eduardo bravely. He started to pick his way down the mud hill.

"Stop!" shouted the Viking, panicking. "I'm stuck! If you move the earth, I'll be buried alive!"

"You will be OK, señor. I am Eduardo Julio Antonio del Monte. I live to free all guinea pigs everywhere, even to free Viking guinea pigs from the mud!" As he spoke, Eduardo slipped. "Oops!"

"Now see what you've done!" The

Viking let loose an angry chatter.
The mud was falling all around him.
Eduardo grabbed the Viking's front
paw as he slid to the bottom, and
pulled him out of danger. They both
landed in a heap. There was the sound
of clapping. All the other guinea
pigs had climbed up to the top of the

mud hill to see what was going on. Sunbeam smiled and waved. Eduardo waved back at her. Coco looked annoyed.

Eduardo let go of the Viking and they both brushed the mud from their fur as best they could.

"And you are . . . ?" asked Eduardo again.

"Muddy," said the Viking, still grumpy.

"Is that a Viking name?"

"No, and it's not my name either. I am Olaf the Ever-Ready."

"Olaf the Oven-Ready?" Eduardo

looked the Viking up and down. "That's a strange name for a guinea pig."

"Are you trying to be funny?" asked the Viking.

Eduardo frowned.

"It's chickens who are oven-ready, Eduardo." Coco slid down the mud hill on her bottom and waggled her paw at him. "Not guinea pigs."

The other guinea pigs slid down after her. Olaf looked around at the group and started counting them as if he were a teacher.

"You've got horns," squeaked

Blossom, the youngest of Banoffee's
children.

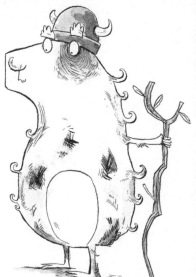

"That's my helmet.
It is made of iron,
and it is from
Norway." Olaf
turned away
and marched
off toward
the stream.
"Follow me."

He even sounded like a teacher.
All of Banoffee's children lined up
in twos, as Banoffee had told them
to do when they were out on school

trips, and followed Olaf. Eduardo, Coco, Fuzzy, Banoffee, and Sunbeam trudged after them.

"You were so brave," whispered Sunbeam to Eduardo.

"It is my duty, señorita. I would do the same for you!" said Eduardo, wiggling his bushy eyebrows.

Coco looked annoyed again.

Olaf walked along the bank of the stream.

"Excuse me," called Fuzzy from the back, "but I think you should know about the builder who's trying to put houses on the thicket."

Olaf ignored him.

"He caused the mudslide with his digger."

Olaf acted as if he hadn't heard.

"He might be back."

"If you have something to say, put your hand up." Olaf stopped at an old wooden hutch. He waited for silence. "This is an original Viking hutch from the ninth century. Note the thatched roof and the mud walls."

They all stopped and looked at the hutch. It didn't look very old. It looked like a twenty-first-century hutch with mud slapped on the walls and grass plonked on the roof.

"Excuse me," said Terry, who liked history almost as much as he liked computers, "but it looks a lot like my hutch. From this century. Only it's dirtier. And it doesn't have Wi-Fi."

Olaf carried on talking: "It is here

in the Great Hall that the weapons, clothes, and jewelry are kept." The visitors looked inside the hutch at a pile of twigs, colored rags, and bits of twisted metal.

"Excuse me," said Banoffee's second youngest, Pepper, putting up her hand, "but are those things really more than a thousand years old? They don't look it."

Olaf didn't answer. He had marched off toward the stream. Everyone else followed. It was exactly like being on a school trip but without the packed lunch.

"And this," said Olaf proudly, "is my longship."

This time no one asked anything. They were all too amazed to speak. Floating on the water was a beautiful long wooden boat, with a dozen oars and a carved dragon at the helm.

"I made it myself. Any questions?"

Lots of hands went up. There were lots of questions. But none of the answers could be heard over a sudden and deafening noise from the other side of the mud hill. A sound that was very, very modern. The digger was back!

7
The Battle of the Thicket

CHUG CHUG CHUG CHUG CHUG!

"By the fur of Freya, what was that?" Olaf looked up in alarm.

"It's the digger!" Fuzzy cried. "I tried to warn you. It's back!"

"BBBUUUURRRRPPPP!"

"And so is the builder, full of fried egg and sausage!" Eduardo held his nose. "Man, that guy stinks! You can smell him a mile away!" He fanned Sunbeam with his satchel.

"Who is this one called Builder?" Olaf demanded.

"Fuzzy already told you!" Coco said impatiently. "This one *called* Builder *is* a builder. That's why we call him it."

"It?" Olaf shouted. "I thought you said his name was Builder."

"It *is* Builder!"

"It and Builder are the same

person?" Olaf asked. "Why didn't you say so?"

"Er . . ." Coco was getting in a terrible muddle.

"It doesn't matter what he's called," Fuzzy said. "The point is, he wants to dig up the thicket and build houses on it. He's got a digger. That's how you got stuck in the mud."

"Best place for you," Coco muttered.

She was getting fed up with Olaf bossing everyone around and being clever and getting all the attention. That was her job normally. "One organized a protest on the Internet to stop him," she boasted.

"No, you didn't! I organized the protest!" Terry objected.

"I think you'll find I did." Eduardo's eyebrows met in a frown.

"I know not of this Internet of which you speak!" Olaf thundered. "But it is clearly no match for the mighty IT. We will have to use stronger weapons."

"Can we make our minds up, please?" Banoffee asked. "Only the kids will need feeding in about half an hour, and then I need to go home and do their hair."

"How about we write a new protest song instead of using weapons?" Sunbeam suggested, gazing at Eduardo.

"A fat lot of good that'll do!" Coco chattered.

"I have an idea, amigos!" Eduardo cried. "I will swing through the air on a branch, land on the builder's head, and eat his eyebrows!"

"Eerrrggg!" Blossom squeaked.

"Yuk!" said Pepper. "What if there's fleas in them? One of my sisters had fleas once. Mom had to pick them out with her teeth."

Banoffee's children all started arguing about which one of them had had fleas.

"Don't all squeak at once!" Olaf shouted. "I'm in charge here!"

"Since when?" Coco asked.

"No one squeaks to Olaf, Viking King of Guinea Pigs, like that!" Olaf glared at her.

"If you're the Viking King of

Guinea Pigs," Coco challenged, "what are you doing in Strawberry Park?"

"I was sent here by the gods over a thousand years ago." Olaf straightened his helmet.

"Rubbish!" Coco chattered. "I don't believe you."

Eduardo frowned at her. Where he

came from, guinea pigs were taught to respect their elders. He stepped forward and bowed. "That is amazing. For I am Eduardo, prince of the Agouti tribe from Peru, sent here by my mother last Easter. I was meant to go to Santa Fe," he explained, "but I got lost."

"Then we must fight together, my brother Eduardo," Olaf cried. "I have many weapons in my Viking hutch. Hands up who is with me?"

Everyone put their hand up except Coco.

"Then come, warriors. Let us prepare for battle against the mighty IT!"

"You go ahead," Coco said sulkily. "I'll stay here and watch the kids."

"Here—" Olaf handed her his helmet. "Keep this, in case IT attacks. And wear this: my Viking lucky charm." He reached forward and pulled it out of the helmet.

"Fine." Coco put them both on.

The helmet wasn't quite her style and the charm necklace looked as if it had been made from candy wrappers. But with her bow, she thought it looked surprisingly pretty.

It didn't take much time for the warriors to get ready. That was partly because there were only six guinea pigs in the army: Eduardo, Fuzzy, Terry, Sunbeam, Banoffee, and Olaf. And it was partly because Olaf's Viking weapon collection turned out to be garbage.

"You sure this isn't a nail?" Terry

whispered, trying out his sword. It was bent. "I think someone's hammered it."

"Dunno," Fuzzy shrugged. "But this shield looks like a rusty old badge."

"I swear this is one of Terry's old hats." Banoffee tried on a woolly helmet. The orange horns drooped.

"I see what you mean," Fuzzy said. "Those are carrots." Someone had nibbled them into the shape of horns and stuck them on!

"Amigos, what do you think of my suit of armor?" Eduardo said in a tinny voice. His head peeped out from one end of a metal cylinder: his feet from the other. He wriggled. "It's a bit tight over my satchel."

"Why does it say 'Baked Beans' on the side?" said Fuzzy suspiciously. He was beginning to doubt whether Olaf really *was* an ancient Viking king. Maybe Coco was right.

At that moment Olaf appeared with

Sunbeam at his side. She was carrying a sign made from a card that said: "Happy 80th Birthday, Grandpa."

"I knew it," Fuzzy muttered. Olaf was bonkers if he thought that was going to frighten anyone.

Before he could say anything, Olaf marched off. "Come, warriors!" he shouted. "This way!"

The five guinea pigs clattered and tripped after him. They went around the bottom of what was left of the mud hill toward the gate to the thicket.

"There IT is!" Olaf shouted.

The builder was working his way with the digger through a clump of long grass near the stream.

"CHARGE!"

Olaf started running toward the digger. The other guinea pigs ran after him, except Eduardo in his baked-bean can, who kept falling over and had to roll.

"I've got a bad feeling about this," Fuzzy panted, bashing at the scoop with his badge.

"Me too!" Terry puffed, prodding at it with the bent nail.

"This is useless!" Banoffee

grumbled, wandering around in circles a little way away. "I can't see a thing! This helmet keeps slipping."

"A little help, amigos!" Eduardo shouted from the baked-bean tin. "I can't get up!"

"Keep fighting!" yelled Olaf, who was standing a safe distance away with Sunbeam, helping her wave the birthday card. "To the death, if necessary!"

"That's easy for you to say," Fuzzy squeaked.

"We can't hold out for much longer!" Terry cried.

CHUG CHUG CHUG CHUG CHUG!

Splash . . . Splash . . . Splash!

"What was that?" Fuzzy puffed. It was coming from the stream.

"Sounded like a fish or something," Terry panted.

SPLASH . . . SPLASH . . . SPLASH!

The sound was getting louder. If it was a fish, it was a very big one!

Just then Fuzzy and Terry saw an amazing sight. The Viking longship was winding its way up the stream, rowed by twelve guinea pigs. At the

far end a thirteenth tiny guinea pig
was shouting, "Pull!" every few
seconds in a high, squeaky voice.

"It's the kids!" yelled Banoffee.
"That's Blossom!"

"And Coco!" cried Fuzzy.

Coco stood at the front of the
longship, wearing Olaf's Viking
helmet and necklace. Her new bow
was tied around one of the horns.
"So much for Olaf the Ever-Ready,"
she snorted. "He's more like Olaf the
Never-Ready!"

The guinea-pig crew giggled.

"Which is why I'm declaring

myself your new Viking Queen," she announced.

Eduardo struggled to his feet. "*Caramba*, princess!" he shouted. "Are we glad to see you!"

8
All Scooped Up

Banoffee stared at the longship in wonder.

"Oh, I am SO proud," she exclaimed. "All my little ones, racing up the river!"

"It's not exactly a race, Mom," said Terry. "They've come to attack the digger."

Banoffee wasn't listening.

"I was proud when I had so many children they could form a full-size football team. I was even prouder when I had so many children they could form a full-size rugby team, as long as I played too. But now I am the proudest I've ever been. The kids can row a longship!"

The longship glided through the

water. The oars looked rather like ice-cream spoons. That's because they were ice-cream spoons, Fuzzy realized.

Coco took a deep breath and led the guinea piglets in song:

Row, row, row the boat,
Gently down the stream . . .

Eduardo looked impressed. "I love that song," he said dreamily.

Sunbeam looked annoyed.

Banoffee's children carefully steered toward the bank of the stream.

"Mind my ship," warned Olaf from the bank. "It's over a thousand years old."

"So how come it's got a remote control?" asked Coco.

"I don't know what you're talking about," muttered Olaf.

Coco lifted a plastic object from the bottom of the longship and held it in the air.

"This is what I'm talking about! I thought it might help us in the battle. What do you think, warriors?" she called out, as she chucked the remote control in the direction of Terry and Fuzzy. They caught it and immediately started to examine the controls.

"Crew!" Coco commanded. "Gather your weapons!"

Banoffee's children each grabbed an oar and a banana skin. (They'd eaten the bananas already, to give them energy.)

"Disembark!"

"My little ones," cried Banoffee, hugging the children one by one as they reached the safety of dry land.

"*Niños!* Children!" called Eduardo to them all. "It is time to stop this digger, once and for all."

"Once and for all!" repeated

Banoffee's children, lifting their oars into the air like swords. Before anyone could stop them, they charged at the digger with their ice-cream-spoon oars raised above their heads.

"I'm not sure what sport they're playing now," said Banoffee, confused.

"It's a bit like hockey," said Terry, making it up as he went along. He didn't want his mother to worry. "Except instead of a stick you have an oar, and instead of a ball you have a digger."

"Wait for me!" cried Coco, chasing after them.

CHUG CHUG CHUG CHUG . . .

The digger moved forward.

DOING!

The digger's scoop dug into the ground.

Banoffee's children ran forward.

Banoffee screamed.

Coco dove for the children.

The scoop twisted in the ground and picked up a pile of earth, several leaves, a lump of chewing gum, a pink hair clip, a five-pence piece, and one end of a worm (unfortunately for the worm). And Banoffee's children. And Coco.

Banoffee fainted.

DUG DUG DUG DUG DUG.

The scoop lifted into the air. It drew level with the window of the driver's cab. The builder moved a lever, which made the scoop tip out its contents, but nothing happened.

He frowned and tried again. Still nothing. While he was staring at the lever, thirteen little faces appeared over the rim of the scoop. Banoffee's kids eyed up the enemy.

"Ready?" came Coco's calm voice from inside the scoop.

"Yup," squeaked Banoffee's kids.

"Steady?"

"Yup."

"FIRE!"

Suddenly a hail of banana skins shot out from the scoop and landed on the window of the driver's cab. The builder looked up. What was going on?

He couldn't see out of
the window!

The builder
jumped down
from the cab and
pulled his phone
from his pocket.

Eduardo
staggered toward
him, looking on in
horror. What was the
builder doing? Calling for help? That
would be a disaster! It was hard
enough fighting just one builder and
one digger. What if more arrived?

Eduardo decided it was time for him to take action. He called out, "*Vamos!* I'm going in!"

"Be careful!" called Coco from the scoop.

Eduardo was still wearing the baked-bean can. It was useless as armor, but it might just work if he pretended he actually *was* a can of baked beans. Especially with a builder who liked breakfast as much as this one did. He tucked his head inside the can. Then he fell over again and rolled toward the digger. He came to a halt just by the cab door. The builder was pacing up and down, talking on the phone.

"Hang on a minute, Mike," the builder said, looking down at what he thought was a can of baked beans. "I think I've just found some more breakfast."

9
Baked Beans Bite Back

"BUURRRPPP!" The builder waddled over to the baked-bean can and prodded it with his boot. "Mmmm!"

Luckily he wasn't the type to notice that the lid was off. Or that the bottom had holes in it. Or that the can had a guinea pig inside it instead of baked beans. All he could think about was his stomach.

He picked up the can and stuck it in his pocket. Then he looked around in amazement.

DUG DUG DUG.

The scoop was going up and down by itself!

"I'm never going back to that useless scrapyard!" he shouted. "They've swindled me with a dodgy digger!"

He got back on the phone and stomped about, shouting.

"Wheeee!" squealed Banoffee's kids. They were having a wonderful time. The scoop was still going up and down.

"I haven't a clue what's going on," Coco muttered.

She was beginning to feel quite dizzy. This wasn't part of her plan. The scoop wasn't just going up and down, it was rocking from side to side too!

"Listen, kids," she said, "I've got to help Eduardo. Wait here until I come get you."

She needn't have worried. The kids

weren't going anywhere. They were having such a great time!

On the next downward lurch Coco leaped out of the scoop and landed safely on the ground next to Olaf and Sunbeam.

WAGGLE WAGGLE. "OOOFFF." *WAGGLE WAGGLE.* "OOOFFF!" Olaf was dancing about, waggling his bottom and making strange noises through his nose. Sunbeam waved the birthday card, looking bored.

"What are you doing now, Olaf?" Coco shouted, heading for the cab.

"By the armpits of Aladdin, I am

praying to the Viking gods to stop the mighty IT!" Olaf shouted. "And see! The gods are smiling on us. That is why the digger is going berserk."

Coco wanted to tell him that

Aladdin wasn't a Viking god and that his silly dance wasn't having any effect on the digger, but he seemed to be having a good time; so she decided to be nice to him for a change. "Keep praying!" she shouted. "I think your dance is working."

Olaf was pleased. "I'll try it this way instead."

He started waggling his nose and making strange noises through his bottom.

WAGGLE WAGGLE. "PARRRP!" *WAGGLE WAGGLE.* "PARRRP!"

Sunbeam fainted.

"Quick, señorita," Coco heard
Eduardo cry from the baked-bean
can. "I'm stuck tighter than an alpaca
in a mouse hole." The builder seemed
so keen on breakfast that Eduardo was
beginning to worry he might actually

eat him even once he found out he wasn't a baked bean.

Coco reached the cab. It was then she realized there was a problem. Well, *another* problem. To get into the cab you had to climb a huge step. And even though Coco could climb, she couldn't get up there. She needed something to wriggle up. What on earth was she going to do? If she didn't act fast, Eduardo would be baked beans on toast.

Suddenly Banoffee sailed through the air past her and landed on the seat in the cab.

"How did you do that?" Coco was astonished.

"It's called *pole vaulting!*" Banoffee said. "I used to do it when I was a kid. I've always loved sports."

"Banoffee, you're brilliant! Tell me what to do," Coco said urgently.

The builder was finishing up his conversation. He put away his phone. *"BUURRRPPP!"* He patted his stomach. Any second now and he'd reach for the baked-bean can!

"Get that twig!" Banoffee pointed to a long bendy stick lying on the ground. "Grab it with both hands."

Coco grabbed the stick with both hands.

"Go back a bit."

Coco went back a bit.

"Now start running."

Coco started running.

"Put the stick in the ground," Banoffee hollered. **"Now . . . jump!"**

Coco felt herself take off. She whizzed through the air and landed in a heap beside Banoffee. Her Viking helmet fell over her eyes.

"Not bad for a beginner." Banoffee gave her a pat.

"Thanks! Now we've got to get Eduardo out!" Coco panted, straightening the helmet.

They felt the digger sag to one side. The builder was climbing back into the cab!

Banoffee and Coco wriggled out of the way as the builder's enormous backside hovered over the seat. He started to pull the baked-bean can from his pocket. Suddenly Coco had an idea. She pulled off her helmet and threw it down.

"Yowwwwwcchhhhh!"

The builder sat on the sharp

Viking horns. He shot up again, jerking the baked-bean can sharply and dislodging Eduardo.

Eduardo flew out of the baked-bean can and landed on the builder's head.

"Aaaarrrrggghhhhh!" The builder screamed. A large black-and-silver guinea pig was eating his eyebrows!

Suddenly the digger lurched forward.

"Are you doing that?" Coco asked Banoffee.

The digger lurched backward.

"No." Banoffee shook her head. "Are you?"

"No!"

Coco and Banoffee slid around on the seat next to the builder. Eduardo clung on with his teeth.

"Who is then?"

"We are!" It was Terry and Fuzzy. They were running about outside the cab. Terry had the remote control for the longship in his paws. They took it in turns to press buttons.

"I told you I could make any remote control work on *anything*!"

Terry laughed. "Although it was Fuzzy's idea," he added generously.

"Get me out of here!" screeched the builder.

The digger stopped suddenly. The builder fell out of the cab.

"Eduardo!" Coco gasped. If the builder had fallen on top of him, he would be flatter than one of Fuzzy's pancakes.

"I'm over here, señorita!"

Coco looked up. Eduardo had catapulted on to a rope some kids had tied to a tree. He was swinging around, picking bits of the builder's eyebrow out of his teeth. Coco couldn't help thinking how handsome he looked.

"Grab hold of this!" Eduardo swung the rope to and fro until the girls could reach it. Coco and Banoffee leaped on. The three guinea pigs slithered down the rope to the ground.

Olaf's Viking dance had come to

an end. He collapsed on the grass, exhausted, next to Sunbeam. "Did we defeat IT?" he gasped.

"Yes, we did," Fuzzy said.

"Now I can die a happy guinea pig and return to my home with the gods!" Olaf's eyes flickered closed.

"Oh, get up, you silly old fool!" Coco gave him a kick. "There's nothing wrong with you. Admit

it, you're not a thousand years old. You're a fake!"

Olaf didn't answer. He was too busy pretending to be dead.

"Never mind, señorita," Eduardo held her paw. "You are our new Viking Queen, remember?"

Coco blushed.

"Well, in that case," she said regally, "one had better congratulate one's warriors. Get the troops out of the scoop, Fuzzy."

Fuzzy and Terry lowered the scoop to the ground with the remote control.

Banoffee's children rushed out,

screaming with excitement.

"That was the best fun EVER!"
shrieked Blossom.

"Can we do it again?" Pepper
squealed.

"You'd better ask your mother," Coco said.

"Where *is* Mom?" asked Terry. "She was awesome with that pole vault."

All the guinea pigs, even Sunbeam and Olaf, looked around for Banoffee.

They froze.

Banoffee was standing a little way away, near the thicket. Next to her was a guinea-pig protester she hadn't seen before. He was big and orange, with pointy ears. Unusually for a guinea pig, he had a long, bushy tail.

"Oh no!" Fuzzy gulped. "It's Renard."

10
Shovel Off!

"My kids aren't frightened of anything or anyone," said Banoffee proudly. "I reckon if they were here now, they wouldn't even cry. I remember once—"

"Excuse me," said the fox, "but could you stop talking so I can eat you?"

Banoffee gave him a disapproving look. "It's rude to interrupt, you know."

"I had to," replied the fox. "Otherwise I wouldn't be able to say anything."

It was true. Banoffee had been talking for some time. This was partly because she always talked a lot about

her kids and partly a tactic to stop the fox from eating her. And it was working.

"You know, I think I'll get out of here and go and live on the railway line," said the fox wearily. "It's covered in nettles, but I'd rather eat nettles than sit here listening to you chattering on."

Banoffee gave him another disapproving look. "You're not very polite, you know."

The fox didn't have a chance to answer because just then he and all the other animals in the thicket heard a human voice. Not the voice of the builder, who was on the phone to Mike again, complaining about his chewed eyebrows, but a woman's voice.

"There's the digger!" It was Henrietta, Coco's owner.

"I don't believe it!" said the man walking next to her. It was Ben, Fuzzy's owner. "The bloggers were right."

The fox loped off to a gap in the fence that led to the railway line. All the other guinea pigs hid in bushes or behind trees or, for the smallest of

Banoffee's children,
under a leaf.

"How dare
they try to
build on this
beautiful
thicket!" said
Henrietta.

"Thank goodness
we read those blogs," said Ben.

The builder was still on the phone
when Ben and Henrietta reached him.
Henrietta tapped him on the shoulder.
He turned around, surprised to see
other people in the thicket.

"You there," said Henrietta firmly, "do you have permission to build on this land?"

"I'll call you back," the builder said, then pocketed his phone. "Sort of," he said, looking shifty.

"I don't believe you," Henrietta snapped.

All the guinea pigs listened carefully to what was said. They didn't understand some of the words, like "council" and "protected land," but they understood the really important ones like "go" and "now." They looked on with glee as the builder climbed back into his cab, turned on the engine, reversed the digger, and drove out of the thicket. They wanted to cheer, but it would alert Ben and Henrietta to the fact that there were twenty guinea pigs hiding in the thicket.

"Let's go and write a comment on the blogs," said Henrietta, "telling everyone the builder has gone."

"While you're doing that, I'll try and stand on my fingers," said Ben.

"Won't that hurt?" asked Henrietta.

"I don't mean stand with my foot on my finger," explained Ben. "I mean

do a finger stand. It's
a yoga position, like a
headstand, but harder."

"Well, good luck with
that," said Henrietta.
"I'll join you when I've
finished on the laptop."

They held hands and
walked off contentedly
toward the house. As
soon as they'd gone all
the guinea pigs came
out from their hiding
places. They clapped

and hugged and Banoffee's children
did a little dance.

"Let's have three cheers for Terry!"
said Fuzzy. "If he hadn't suggested the

blog the builder would still be here. Just shows what good the Internet can do. Hip hip . . ."

"Hang on," said Terry, as everyone was taking a breath, ready to give a loud cheer, "it's not all down to me. If Fuzzy hadn't been so clever with the remote control, the kids might still be in that scoop."

"That's true," said Blossom, "although it was quite fun."

"Yes, but it was dangerous too," said Banoffee.

"So let's have three cheers for Terry," said Fuzzy. "Hip hip . . ."

"Just a minute," said Coco loudly, "but I think you'll find it was all down to me dressing up as a Viking Queen, leading the longship, organizing the children, and putting the helmet under the builder's bottom."

"Señors and señoritas," said Eduardo wisely, "let us cheer for everyone, for we all played a part in the famous Viking Battle of the Thicket. Hip hip . . ."

And they all cheered.

When the cheering had died down, Olaf asked in a small voice, "Can I have my remote control back?"

"Of course," said Terry, handing it over.

"You're not a thousand years old, are you?" said Fuzzy quietly.

"No," said Olaf sadly. "But I do know an awful lot about history. That's why I like pretending."

"I've got an idea," said Sunbeam unexpectedly. "Why don't you offer visits to the model Viking settlement here in the thicket, complete with longship ride?"

Everyone turned and looked at Sunbeam. They'd more or less forgotten about her, perhaps because she'd been passed out most of the time.

"That's a really good idea," Terry said. "You could charge three lettuce leaves for students and a cucumber slice for under-twelves."

"I could help you," Sunbeam offered. "That is, if nobody minds." She looked at Coco.

"By the hair of Hercules, that would be fantastic!" Olaf cried.

"I'll bring the kids!" smiled Banoffee.

"Of course we don't mind!" Coco squeezed Sunbeam's paw. She was glad they were all going to be special friends after all.

If you had taken a stroll around Strawberry Park that evening you would have seen:

Banoffee's kids rowing down the stream in the longship with Olaf and Sunbeam;

Banoffee using the free time to braid her fur;

Eduardo writing a song about the Viking Battle of the Thicket;

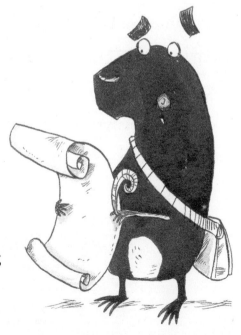

Ben and Henrietta
in the garden
telling their
neighbors about
the protest blogs;

and, later on, Fuzzy and Coco, on
their owners' knees, full of juicy green
grass and very happy after their
exciting, boring, scary, silly, funny,
and very, very tiring day.

the end

Be Safe Online!

Surfing the internet is lots of fun, but there are some things Coco and Fuzzy want you to remember so that you stay safe online . . .

GUINEA PIGS ONLINE

G is for *Go Away!*
Never chat online with people you don't know. Never reply to messages from people you don't know. Finally, never, ever agree to meet up with someone you have only met online—it could be dangerous!

P is for *Private!*
Never tell anyone your personal information, like where you live, your phone number, or your passwords. It's your private information and that's how it should stay—private.

O is for *Oh Really?*
You really can't trust everything you read on the internet. Check any information you learn online with an adult to make sure it's true—you might be surprised how much false information is out there!

L is for *Let an Adult Know*
Finally, you should always let an adult know about what you're doing on the internet. And if you're worried about something that you've seen or read online, tell a grown-up right away—adults can be really good at explaining things that might seem mysterious to you.

You're much better at using the Internet than Coco is . . .

. . . so why not visit

www.guinea-pigs-online.com

for lots more fun, giggles and squeaks
with your favorite furry pals!

about the authors and illustrator

Jennifer Gray is a lawyer. She lives in central London and Scotland with her husband, four children, and an overfed cat, Henry. Jennifer's other books for children include a comedy series about Atticus Claw, the world's greatest cat burglar.

Amanda Swift has written for several well-established children's TV series, including *My Parents Are Aliens*; she has also written three novels for middle-grade readers: *The Boys' Club*, *Big Bones*, and *Anna/Bella*. She lives in southeast London, near the Olympic park. Unlike Coco, she hasn't met the queen.

Sarah Horne was born in Stockport, Cheshire, on a snowy November day, and grew up scampering in the fields surrounding Buxton, Derbyshire. She is propelled by a generous dose of slapstick, a love for color and line, a clever story, and a good cup of coffee.